CALL GIRL

AN EROTIC ADVENTURE

VICTORIA RUSH

VOLUME 39

JADE'S EROTIC ADVENTURES - BOOK 39

COPYRIGHT

For the uninhibited...

WANT TO AMP UP YOUR SEX LIFE?

Sign up for my newsletter to receive more free books and other steamy stuff. Discover a hundred different ways to wet your whistle!

Victoria Rush Erotica

1

After another long day of boring client meetings, I felt exhausted. It was hard enough staying focused all the time trying to demonstrate my value. But the worst part was always having to keep my game-face on to protect my professional standing. I had a longstanding policy about not fraternizing with my clients. After an earlier office affair had gone bad and my more influential partner had blocked me from further promotions, I vowed never again to mix business with pleasure.

When I got back to my hotel room, I kicked off my heels and flopped down onto the bed, exhaling deeply at the chance to finally let down my guard and relax. I'd chosen to treat myself on this business trip to Washington DC with an upgrade to the St. Regis Hotel using my accumulated Marriott reward points. Only two blocks from the White House, it was perfectly situated for me to make the rounds of all the power centers where I'd carefully cultivated business relationships over the years.

Sumptuously appointed with all the features of a world-class hotel, it had everything a weary business traveler could want. Whether it was their fully-equipped health club with large swimming pool, an in-house spa for facials or massages, or my choice of three five-star restaurants, I hardly had to leave the hotel to satisfy any personal needs. But today, I was feeling in need of some *other* personal services. After suffering through eight hours of stuffy meetings with fat overweening executives, I was feeling the need for a sexy young body next to me. One who I could suck up to in a whole *different* kind of way.

After calming my mind and letting my blood pressure return to normal, I had a long hot shower then opened my travel bag to see what outfits I'd packed for more leisurely pursuits. I pulled out a tight mid-thigh red dress with low-cut decolletage, and after pairing it with black Christian Louboutin heels with matching red lacquer soles, I turned around admiring myself in the full-length dressing mirror.

You still got it, girl, I smiled to myself, appraising my tight ass and full breasts spilling over the neckline of my dress. For a thirty-six-year-old, I still had the lithe figure of someone ten years younger than my age. After curling my shoulder-length hair and adding some dark eye shadow and matching red lipstick, I grabbed my gold-colored clutch and headed downstairs to the main floor bar. When I entered the elegantly-appointed room, I noticed a group of older gentlemen sitting in a corner lounge eyeing me up while I strolled over to the bar to take a seat in one of the raised chairs.

Great, I sighed to myself. *Just what I need right about now. Another group of pudgy old business executives leering at me from the other side of the room.*

Seeing my discomfort sitting on the raised pedestal like an exotic bird on display in a zoo, the bartender approached me with a warm smile.

"Welcome to the Regis Bar," he said, placing a coaster on the counter in front of me. "Can I get you something to drink?"

"Grey Goose martini, please," I said. "With three olives."

"The more the merrier," he chuckled, turning to prepare my cocktail.

I peered in the mirror pretending to check my messages on my phone and noticed a younger couple staring at me out of the corner of their eyes. I must have been quite a sight dressed up in my candy-apple-red dress with bare shoulders, teetering on the edge of my stool with my long legs dangling over the edge. As I fantasized about taking them up to my room, I squirmed in my chair, feeling the heat beginning to emanate between my crossed legs.

The bartender returned with my martini, and just as I raised one of the olives to my mouth, a handsome hunk wearing a perfectly tailored suit entered the room from the lobby side of the hotel, meeting my gaze in the mirror. Without skipping a beat, he walked calmly up to the bar and took a seat immediately to my left.

"Good evening," he said, motioning for the bartender to bring him a drink.

"It's getting there," I purred, rolling the olive around in my mouth as I smiled back at him.

He took a quick glance at my tight-fitting outfit, then peered back at me with smoldering gray eyes.

"Did you plan that on *purpose*, or are always perfectly coordinated with your surroundings?"

"What do you mean?" I said, not entirely sure where he was going.

"Your *dress*," he said, peering around the room at the bright decor. "The red and gold motif. Didn't you notice how well it complimented the decoration of this place?"

"Not until you mentioned it," I smiled, suddenly noticing the resemblance. "Don't you like it? Should I change?"

"*God* no," he said. "It's perfect. Please don't change a damn thing."

The bartender arrived and nodded toward the gentleman.

"Good evening, sir. Would you something to drink?"

The man peered over at me sucking on another olive balanced on the end of a plastic skewer, shifting uncomfortably on his chair.

"That looks mouthwatering," he said. "What are you having?"

"A Grey Goose martini, straight up."

"I like the sound of that," he said. "But I usually prefer mine dirty."

"So do I," I cooed. "It's just tonight I felt the need to suck on something hard and juicy."

"Dirty it is then," the man said, clearing his throat as he nodded toward the bartender.

Trying to suppress a knowing smirk, he turned around and headed back to the other side of the bar.

"I'm Dane," the man said, extending a well-muscled arm and immaculately manicured hand toward me.

"Jade," I said, placing my hand in his as he squeezed me softly.

"That's a name you don't hear too often," he smiled, lingering a bit longer than usual with his handhold.

"Mmm," I nodded, not yet ready to inform him it wasn't my real name but a nickname I'd adopted not long after divorcing my husband when I began dating anonymously again. "I suppose so. But I'm getting used to it."

"Shouldn't you be wearing something green to compliment that feature of you also?" he said, brushing my hair gently aside to peer at my earrings.

"Do my *eyes* count?" I said, pulling back slightly to rebuff his advance. As hot as he was, I wanted to make it clear that I wasn't going to fall into his arms as easily as all the other conquests he'd undoubtedly bedded employing his intoxicating charms.

"Absolutely," he said, sitting back in his chair and taking a large swig of his murky martini. "So what brings you to these parts on this cool autumn day?"

"Just looking for a little adventure," I said coyly, still playing hard to get, not wanting to give him too many details. After changing into sexy evening wear, the last thing I wanted to talk about was *work*. "This looked like a nice enough place to meet some interesting candidates."

"Indeed it is," Dane said, taking a more measured sip of his martini.

I took a moment to appraise his handsome face and shapely build, having little doubt he'd picked up many other lonely wayfarers with his impressive package of assets. His hair was thick and wavy with a light dusting of hair gel, keeping it perfectly tousled atop his head. His nose was strong but straight, and his jaw was smooth and bereft of any sign of five-o'clock-shadow, like he'd just shaved in anticipation of going on the prowl. He was definitely a looker, but there was something about his perfect countenance that seemed a bit off.

"How about you?" I said. "You look like you fit in pretty well in this power-hungry city yourself."

"I don't know about *that*," he smiled. "But I try to play the part. I'm a lobbyist."

"Ah," I nodded. "That explains your perfectly manicured

look. I bet you're pretty successful getting your way with the targeted prospects."

"I have my occasional conquests," he said, calmly gulping down the rest of his martini.

I glanced down toward his crotch and noticed one side of his trousers tenting from an obvious erection.

"I bet you do," I smiled.

"Do you want to get out of this stuffy joint and go somewhere more comfortable?" he said, realizing we were thinking the same thing.

"Sure," I said, tipping my martini glass and bobbing the last olive in and out of my lips suggestively. "Your place or mine?"

"I live in Georgetown, but I'm not sure I'm going last that long."

"I've got a room upstairs if that suits your fancy better."

"Yes," he said, placing a crisp fifty-dollar-bill on the counter to cover the cost of our two overpriced martinis. "The less distance between you and that amazing body, the better."

He stood up and held out his hand to help me off the chair, then he slid his hand behind the small of my back as we walked briskly toward the elevator bank in the lobby. When we got in the first open lift and the door closed in front of us, he lifted me up by my armpits and pressed me against the hard wood paneling, pushing my dress high above my hips while thrusting his hardening manhood against my burning pussy.

Normally, I didn't jump into bed with someone this quickly, but there was something about this hunk that reeked of sex and I wanted him just as badly as he evidently wanted me. But as soon as our lips met and I plunged my tongue deep down his throat, the elevator doors suddenly opened to my eighth-floor hallway where an older couple stood dressed in expensive evening wear eyed us disapprovingly.

"Don't mind us," Dane said, stretching my dress down and leading me out of the elevator as we breezed past the alarmed couple. "We're newlyweds. You remember those days, don't you?"

As we stumbled down the hallway in the direction of my guestroom, I fumbled for my keycard. As soon as I unlatched the door, he carried me toward the bed, practically flinging me on top of it. I wasn't used to being treated so rough, but with this sexy Adonis, I was more than happy to be his plaything for one night. As he began to rip off his tie and throw his suit on the back of my side chair, I pulled my dress over my shoulders and kicked my heels to the side of my bed near the nightstand.

Seeing me lying almost naked on the bed and waiting for him, he hopped on each foot as he removed his socks, then he pounced on the bed beside me, clutching at my bra and panties to remove my last stitches of clothing. Expertly unclasping my bra with one hand, he simultaneously pulled my panties down my legs with his other. I grabbed his package over his boxer-brief underwear, gasping at how thick and hard his pole felt still constrained by the tight cotton.

When he pulled them down over his hips and his organ flapped free, my eyes gaped at how thick and large he was. Easily ten inches long and three inches thick, it was the biggest dick I'd seen on a man in a long time. Normally, I was perfectly happy being penetrated by my favorite sex toys or the strap-on dildo of my lesbian lovers, but tonight I was dripping in anticipation of feeling a real flesh-and-blood cock pounding inside me.

I reached down and circled his iron-hard shaft with my right hand, squeezing it as tightly as I could. Hardly making a dent in his engorged flesh, he began pumping it in and out of my fist while sucking on my hardening nipples like a child just given his first lollypop. His technique was a bit rough, but by now I was so worked up and in need of a good fucking, he probably could have planted me on his pole and spun me around a couple of times to get me off.

When I tried to move my body down lower to take his erection in my mouth, he placed his hand under my jaw and lifted my face, placing his lips firmly against mine as our tongues danced wildly in each other's mouths. Then he rolled over on top of me and pulled my legs up over my hips, placing the crown of his cock over my dripping slit. I could feel his own lubrication mingling with mine as he paused for a moment pressing my folds apart, then he rammed the full length of his hard-on inside me in one fell swoop.

I grunted in a combination of surprise and delight as he began humping me noisily from the wetness of our conjoined parts slapping together hungrily. I hadn't been fucked this hard by anybody in a long time, and I relished the feeling of lying helplessly under his powerful body while he had his way with me. I could feel the sweat building up between his hard pecs and my compressed tits as he slid his body up and down my torso with long, powerful strokes.

As I grunted and moaned in rising pleasure from the feeling of his huge cock inside me, he raised his face briefly from mine and peered at me with a lustful look.

"Yeah?" he mocked. "You like that? You like it when I fuck you hard?"

"Yes," I panted. "Pound my pussy with your giant dick. I

want to feel you spurting your firehouse inside me when I squirt all over your balls..."

"Fuck yes," he said, temporarily pulling out of me and flopping me over with my glistening ass pointing up toward his flagpole.

I half expected him to ram his poker into my asshole, but instead he spread my legs a few inches apart while I tilted my hips up in the air expectantly.

"Yes, Dane," I purred. "Fuck me from behind. I want to feel your big balls slapping up against my ass."

He positioned his knees on either side of my ass then he pointed his monster toward my dripping hole. As I felt him begin to fill me up, he lowered his body on top of mine, almost smothering me in the thick duvet atop my luxurious bedspread. He intertwined his fingers with mine, then pulled them up over my head as he slid his body over mine while humping my ass. The feeling of his huge instrument pounding me from behind while he pinned my body underneath was incredibly arousing, and I groaned in tandem with him as I listened to his passion rising.

Just as I began to feel my body tightening in preparation for my rapidly approaching my orgasm, he lurched one last time hard against my ass, squeezing my hands tightly as he pressed his cock deep into my pussy, spurting all over my convulsing cervix. When I felt him coming inside me, my pussy clamped down hard over his phallus while I squirted juices out the side of my stretched slit over the sides of his quivering thighs and sweaty balls.

He held me for a few minutes in this constrained position until we both finished jerking and spasming, then with the same paucity of drama he began with, he pulled out of me and flopped onto the mattress beside me. I hadn't been fucked this hard without remorse in a long time, but somehow I found the experience insanely erotic and arousing. As I began to feel his sputum seeping out of my hole onto the expensive bedding, I excused myself to use the washroom.

When I returned a few minutes later, I found that he'd disappeared with all of his belongings, leaving no trace of what had just happened other than the tumbled and disheveled bed linens that looked like a herd of wildebeest had just trampled over them. As I reached to grab a swig of water from the complimentary bottle on my side table, I noticed a bundle of crisp one-hundred-dollar bills resting on my nightstand.

At first, I looked at the money in shock, hardly believing what I was seeing. It was obvious that he thought I was a hooker hitting him up for business at the bar, and I couldn't blame him, tarted up the way I was and flirting with him unapologetically.

But a *prostitute*? Did I really look like a *hooker*?

As I stood looking down at the money dumbfounded, my brow suddenly began to pinch, curious to see how much he thought I was worth.

I sat down on the bed and slowly lifted the bills off the table, fanning them apart to count my ill-gotten prize. As I gaped at the loot like I'd just won the jackpot in a game of five-card-stud, I shook my head when I realized he'd left me a cool five hundred bucks for our quick one-night stand.

2

———

For most of the following day, I could hardly concentrate in my client meetings thinking about what had happened last night. On the one hand, I was horrified to think someone I picked up in a bar thought I was a hooker. But the amount he'd paid me for a quick roll in the sack was more than I typically made during a full day of regular work. And having sex with a hot young stud was a lot more fun than slaving over a design commission with another boring client.

When I got back to my hotel room, I paused for a moment looking at myself in the mirror. Although I found the idea of earning money for anonymous sex an incredible turn-on, it all had a slightly unsavory feel to it. But the more I thought about it, the more I began to think the amount I'd been paid for my time undervalued my services. I'd heard street-corner hookers earned fifty bucks for a quick blow job, but I was a far cry from a typical streetwalker. I sat down on my bed and popped open my laptop, punching in the search phrase *what is the going rate for high-end call girls?*

I was surprised to find that elite escort agencies charged

anywhere from one to ten thousand dollars per client. *What the fuck?* I thought, raising my eyebrows in shock. *I'm charging less than half that amount sucking up to pretentious executives who already treat me like I'm their personal slave. I'd rather make twice the amount of money working for one-tenth the amount of time, doing something I enjoy!*

I snapped my laptop shut then opened my travel bag to see what other clothing I'd packed for evening entertainment. If I could make five hundred bucks without really trying, I wondered how much could I earn if I played a little harder to get and chose my marks more carefully. But when I flipped through my suitcase, I was disappointed to see that all the other clothes I'd packed besides my business suits were frumpy old blouses and jeans. Nothing else came close to matching my tight red, candy-apple-colored dress for screaming *look at me – I'm hot and available for a quick pick-up!*

After donning my outfit and touching up my makeup, I peered back in the mirror and smiled. Yes, I was about to prostitute myself again, this time intentionally, but at least I'd do it on my own terms. I'd take my time choosing my marks, aiming for a more discerning client. Someone who'd be willing to pay me closer to my real worth. After all, I said to myself, performing sex for money was the world's oldest profession, one with a never-ending line of customers wanting to get laid. I was simply fulfilling the natural need of any red-blooded man or woman. The fact that I was about to get *paid* for my services was just icing on the cake.

When I reentered the lobby bar and took a seat at the counter, the bartender noticed me wearing the same red dress and smiled. I'd considered going slightly further afield to flaunt my wares, but the Regis Bar was only a quick elevator ride back to my working lair, and if it had one thing going for it, it was that anyone that could afford to eat, drink, or stay in this establishment was probably loaded with plenty of extra spending money. So *what* if I was wearing the same tarty red dress two nights in a row? This was a *hotel*—most of the patrons were just passing through and wouldn't notice anyway.

I sat down on my stool and ordered my usual martini, then slowly scanned the room in the smoky mirror behind the bottles stacked on the other side of the bar. There was the usual scattering of business executives chatting in the lounges on the far wall, a few older couples sipping cocktails at separate tables, and a handsome middle-aged man pretending not to notice me as he flipped through his mobile phone.

The older couples peered at me sternly, like I was some kind of tackily wrapped Christmas gift positioned at the front of the tree for prime plucking, which I suppose in a way, I was. But I noticed the husbands lingered a little longer than their blue-haired wives, darting their eyes up and down my long legs dangling over the edge of my stool.

I tried to make eye contact with some of the serious-looking business executives, but they seemed more intent on plying their seatmates for extra work than approaching me for some extra-curricular fun. But the lone gentleman seemed slightly more interested in me, and I noticed him peering up periodically, trying not to be too obvious. When our eyes finally met, he smiled and nodded gently, as if to say 'I see you and I think you're fine.'

I bobbed my foot playfully on my knee, slurping on the olives in my drink as I had the night before, and before long he placed his phone down on his table, giving me all my attention. When my martini was almost finished, the bartender suddenly approached me, sliding a fresh one across the counter.

"From the gentleman in the corner," he smiled. "With his compliments."

I gulped down the rest of my drink then lifted the new glass and turned toward the gentleman, nodding my appreciation. He smiled back at me and tilted his head, motioning for me to join him at his table. I paused for a moment contemplating his offer, then swung back around, pretending to ignore his supplications. But as I continued sipping my martini, my eyes flitted back up and down periodically, teasing him with my shy-girl act while I swiveled playfully on my stool.

After a few more minutes, the bartender slid another martini across the counter toward me, telling me that the gentleman had paid for it again. We continued our little cat-and-mouse routine for another fifteen minutes or so, until I began to feel the effects of the three martinis starting to make me tipsy. When he motioned for me to join him again at his table, I lowered myself off my tall stool and wobbled toward the plush armchairs at his table, happy to rest my teetering body on a more comfortable chair.

"Good evening," he said in a confident tone when I reached his table. "You looked like you might need some company. You're far too pretty to be spending your time alone in a place like this."

"Is there something *wrong* with this place?" I said, sinking down into the deeply upholstered chair, happy to be taking the weight off my unsteady legs.

"Not usually," he said. "It's just that you kind of stand out among all these preening politicians and blue-haired tourists. Kind of like a newborn fawn surrounded by a pack of hungry wolves."

"Really," I said, taking another sip of my martini. "I

hadn't noticed. Everybody seemed pretty wrapped up in their own conversation."

"Well, I'm pretty sure they weren't talking about the latest policy initiative or which museum they wanted to visit next. You're a pretty compelling attraction all on your own."

"Not quite as impressive as the Lincoln or Jefferson Memorial, I imagine," I said, tugging on the lower hem of my dress as I crossed my bare legs.

The man took a long look at my exposed skin and shook his head.

"Oh, I'm pretty sure you'd have no difficulty maintaining the interest of many a wayward traveler for just as long as those other luminaries."

"I've never been mentioned in such distinguished company," I chuckled. "What about you? Are you here to see the sights or do some business?"

"A little bit of both," he said, crossing his knees with the toe of his shoe resting a few inches away from my own. "I'm a lawyer, so I'm always on the lookout for potential new engagements."

"It looks like you've already *crossed* that divide," I said, noticing the ring on the third finger of his left hand.

"Oh this?" he said, twisting the band slowly with the fingers of his other hand. "This is merely *symbolic* at this point in our relationship. My wife and I have an under-standing."

"An *understanding*?" I said, raising an eyebrow. "And do your, um, *other* lady friends have a similar understanding?"

"If the price is right, we all eventually come to a mutual understanding."

"Everything's about money and power in this town," I scoffed, shaking my head.

"Not *everything*," he said, glancing down at my breasts spilling over the top of my dress.

"So, what was your plan?" I said. "To liquor me up until my willpower was sufficiently whittled down?"

"Something like that."

"Well, three martinis is pretty much my upper limit. Otherwise, I'm liable to lie down for reasons other than my own free will."

"We can't have that," he said. "You're far too interesting to make love to any other way than fully conscious."

"Are you *always* this direct with the target of your desires?" I said, cocking my head to the side.

"Only the most attractive ones."

"But I haven't promised anything yet."

"I think you put all your cards on the table when you began flirting with me at the bar and accepted my invitation to join me at my table."

"I'm not that easy," I said, crossing my arms defiantly.

"I'm sure you're not," he smiled. "But I can make it worth your while."

"With another one of your legal accommodations?" I said, dancing around his increasingly transparent proposition on the table.

"Yes, but with fair consideration on both sides. A contract isn't legally binding without proper incentive from both parties."

"You make it sound so *contractual*."

"That's what you wanted isn't it?" he said. "Unless I've misjudged the signals..."

I paused for a moment to appraise my potential paramour. He definitely had all the pieces I looked for in a partner. Wit, intelligence, good looks, and a certain sexual energy about him. I was tempted to ask him how much he was willing to pay to take me to my room, but that seemed a little too trailer park for my sensibilities. Plus, the tables in the lounge were too close together for me to make such a bold and potentially dangerous proposal.

"I've got a room upstairs if you think you can make it worth my while," I said softly.

"Oh, I'm pretty sure I can make it worth your while," he said with a sly smile.

"Shall we consummate the deal then?" I said, continuing our legal metaphor.

He pulled out his wallet and lay a hundred-dollar bill on the table to cover the costs of both of our drinks, then he held out his hand to help me off my chair. I was happy for the extra support with the effects of the three martinis beginning to make my brain feel like it was floating around in a goldfish bowl. When we got into the closed elevator, this time there were no wild histrionics, only his gentle holding of my hand as we waited for the lift to reach my floor with my heart thumping heavily in my chest. I could scarcely believe I was about to do this again, this time with *both* of us clear about the terms of engagement. It felt vaguely immoral, but at the same time incredibly exciting.

When we stepped into my guestroom and closed the door, he led me to my bed where he began to undress me slowly and gently. It was a refreshing change to have my partner treat me like a lady, and I could feel my panties beginning to dampen as I peered into his steely eyes. Well-tanned with perfectly groomed salt-and-pepper hair, he reminded me of the suave and sexy manner of George Clooney. As he unzipped the back of my dress and began to pull it down over my shoulders, I leaned in toward him to kiss him gently on the lips.

I might have been a hooker-for-hire in his eyes, but that

didn't mean I couldn't enjoy the transaction and add a little intimacy to our brief encounter. He raised his right hand to the side of my head, brushing his fingers gently through my hair as we kissed softly, interlocking our lips and tasting the wetness in each other's mouths. As my dress dropped to the floor, I stepped forward and kicked off my heels, and he reached around my back and unclasped my bra, placing it gently on a nearby chair.

"I like your style," I mewed, raising my chest to show off my firm, plump breasts.

"I like *yours* too," he said, reaching out to roll my nipples between the fingers of both hands while he stared straight into my eyes.

His calm, confident manner was getting me more turned on by the minute, and while he continued playing with my breasts, I began unfastening his tie and unbuttoning his shirt in an equally slow, sensuous manner. When I pulled open his shirt, I was surprised to see how lean and ripped he was under his clothes, belying his obvious age. This was someone who obviously took care of himself and anyone else he came into contact with, and I was eager to avail myself of his other talents.

After I removed his shirt and threw it on the chair next to my bra, he began unbuckling his belt, then he slowly pulled his pants down and folded them over the edge of the chair. When he pulled off his socks and underwear, I paused for a moment admiring his tanned and trim physique with his half-erect penis pushing over to one side of his thigh. His cock wasn't as large as the hunk from last night, but there was something about its caramel-colored tanned perfection that made me want to take it into my mouth.

I sunk to my knees and placed his dick in my mouth, rolling my tongue over the slippery surface of his head as I began to feel it swell and harden. Within fifteen seconds or so, he was fully erect, and I cupped his balls, playing with them softly as he purred contentedly above me. But as his purrs soon changed into groans with his balls beginning to elevate in rising passion, he clasped my head gently and turned my face up toward him while peering down at me with his cock impaled in me like an arrow embedded in the bullseye of a hay bale.

"I'd rather make love to you," he said, lifting me up with one finger under my chin. "Take off your panties. Let me see *all* of you."

I reached under the waistband of my panties and pulled them down the length of my legs, then stepped out of them, placing them over the wooden arm of the adjacent chair.

The man took a step back, silently appraising my body from head to toe. He didn't have to say a single word: his bobbing cock did all the talking. It was obvious he was attracted to me, and I could feel a trickle of lubrication running down the inside of one thigh as I watched his chest rising and falling in appreciation. Then he grabbed my hand and pulled down a corner of the bedsheets, laying me delicately on the mattress.

I hadn't been made love to so gently by another man in a long time, and my pussy fluttered in excitement at his gentlemanly approach. When he lay down beside me and rolled toward me, I could feel the wetness of his precum on my thigh, and when he felt my lubrication mingling with his own, he leaned forward, kissing me firmly on my mouth. This time, his tongue pressed my lips apart while he caressed the underside of my flesh, and I moaned at his deft and sensual touch. If this was how he approached all of his legal arrangements, I had no doubt he was one of the top lawyers in town.

While he continued kissing me softly, his left hand circled my breast, cupping and squeezing it gently as he rolled my nipple between his fingers like it was some kind of exotic fabric. I groaned in his mouth, lifting one of my legs to wrap around his ass, hoping he'd move his cock closer to my aching pussy. But instead of engaging me in the standard missionary position, he gently pressed me down onto the mattress and lifted my leg until the side of my ass pressed against his flaring cock. Then he pressed his pole between my splayed legs, rubbing its entire length against my dripping slit, pausing to rub his searing crown against my clit while he continued to kiss me and caress my breasts.

Fuck me, I thought. *This guy really knows how to make love to a woman.* For a briefest of moments, I wondered if he'd been the first man I made love to if I'd ever have wandered into the arms of another woman again.

"Are you this good at *everything* you do?" I panted, flapping my hips against his, trying to gain more traction on my burning clit.

"Only the things that give me and my partner this much pleasure," he said.

"If this is what you call fair and appropriate consideration, maybe *I'm* the one who should be paying you for your services."

"I'm pretty sure we're *both* going to get our just rewards from our little arrangement tonight," he said.

After thoroughly coating his cock with the wetness pouring out of my slit while he stroked my pussy seductively up and down, he angled his hips backward a few inches then pointed his throbbing pecker directly into my hole, pausing at the entrance to tease me mercilessly.

"Yes," I panted, rocking my hips forward and back impatiently. "Please fuck me. I need you to execute the contract directly, or whatever you lawyers call it."

"Mmm," he grunted, slowly beginning to penetrate me with his thick dick. "You're not like most of my other business conquests."

"Oh?" I panted as he began to slide his whole length inside me. "Because I'm a little juicier than your other partners?"

"No," he said, beginning to squeeze my breasts more firmly. "Because you seem to *enjoy* the exchange more than the others."

Even though I suspected he was no longer talking about his *legal* partners so much as other women he'd bedded, it didn't seem to bother me that he was comparing me to other hookers he'd been with.

"Maybe it's because you're so good at what you do," I purred. "Like you said, the most successful contracts are ones where the consideration is equally attractive on both sides."

"Damn, girl," he said, embracing my shoulders as he began to penetrate me more deeply. "You could make a lawyer want to hang up his diploma to pursue other professions. You're not like the other girls–"

"Other *call* girls, you mean?" I said, pressing my breasts against his chest as he continued to kiss me more passionately.

"Like *any* woman I've been with," he grunted. "Though I must admit you seem to have found your calling..."

"This isn't my usual job," I said. "I just do this for a little extra entertainment while I'm visiting with my *real* clients."

"Well, feel free to visit me any time you're in town," he grunted, beginning to tighten his hold on my shoulders.

From the sound of his escalating breathing and the pace

of his stroking, I knew he was getting near the peak of his pleasure. With my own pleasure ramping up in tandem from his expert lovemaking, I reached around behind me and clasped his balls in my hand, squeezing them gently.

"Come for me, baby," I purred. "I want to feel your balls when you cum inside me. Help me create *two* satisfied parties to this contract."

"Unnh," the man groaned, obviously enjoying my attention on his tightening testicles. "You're making this impossible for me to hold out much longer..."

"There's no need," I panted with him. "I'm almost there. Take me over the edge. Let me feel you throbbing inside me."

I extended my little finger toward his anus and caressed the area under his balls, tickling the soft fur of his perineum, then I felt his perineal muscle begin flexing in the telltale sign of powerful orgasm.

"Nnnnn," he grunted in a long growl, pressing his hard pubis tightly against my pussy as I began squirting over the base of his dick and my hand gripping his balls.

As we both squealed into each other's mouths in a passionate embrace, our bodies pressed together in one final protracted spasm while we held each other tightly. When we both finally relaxed our grip and fell back upon the mattress, the man stayed inside me, gently kissing the sides of my mouth and neck.

"I could do this all night," he panted contently. "Are you willing to execute a few *more* contracts this evening?"

"As long as there's fair and appropriate consideration on both sides," I smiled.

Two hours later, the man calmly got dressed and kissed me on the cheek, laying a neat stack of bills on my night table along with his card.

"I have no idea who you are," he said. "But I sure hope you look me up the next time you're in town."

"I hadn't really planned on doing this much longer," I smiled. "But after tonight, you've made me reconsider what I want to do for a living."

After he let himself out, I sat down on the bed and counted the money. It wasn't so much that I *needed* it as it was a way of measuring my worth and judging how good he thought I was in bed. As I separated the bills and placed them individually upon my nightstand, I smiled when I saw that the man had left me a cool thousand dollars for another night's work.

3

Going back to my regular job the next day was even harder than it had been the day before. As much as I'd enjoyed my rough and tumble roll in the hay with the young stud two nights ago, somehow last night's encounter with the handsome older gentleman was even more exciting. This time, we'd *both* gone into it fully aware that it would be a business transaction, and yet I'd enjoyed the sex as much as ever. 'Turning tricks' wasn't nearly as sordid and unpleasant as I'd heard. In fact, if every john I picked up was as smooth and skilled as the man from last night, I could quickly get used to this new part-time vocation. The fact that my pay scale seemed to be rapidly escalating along with my enjoyment of the experience was just icing on the cake.

For the rest of the day, I went through the motions pretending to pay attention during the never-ending client meetings, then I rushed back to my hotel when our business was finished, excited to see what new surprises I might uncover in the mysterious downstairs room this evening.

When I entered the bar again in my customary outfit, the bartender greeted me with a knowing smile.

"The usual?" he said after I parked myself in the same stool.

"Yes please," I said.

In my zealousness to rush downstairs as soon as possible, the bar was quieter than usual this early in the evening, and it took a couple of hours for it to begin filling with suitable prospects. There was the usual smattering of gray-suited political types and touristy couples visiting the capital from out of town, but I was interested in sampling something a little different this evening.

Around eight o'clock, I noticed the same young couple from two nights ago come into the room and take a table a few degrees to my left. As I sipped my cocktail trying to play it cool, I noticed them peering up at me frequently while they whispered quietly amongst themselves. The girl was cute and perky in a high-school-cheerleader kind of way, with long blond hair and skinny jeans and a tight t-shirt that showed off her curvy, athletic figure. Her boyfriend looked to be about the same age, barely in his early twenties, with tousled brown hair and a cute smile.

Definitely fuckable, I thought, squirming on my chair.

It had been almost two weeks since I'd felt the soft skin of another naked woman lying next to me, and I was definitely ready for a little change of pace tonight. After the three of us exchanged a few playful glances in the bar mirror, the couple rose from their table and walked toward me, talking a stool on either side of me.

"Hi," the girl said, twisting her chair toward me.

"Hi," I replied, just as cheerily.

"If you don't mind my saying," she said. "My husband

and I have been watching you and we just wanted to tell you how beautiful you are."

"You're quite a handsome couple *yourself*," I said, turning to smile at the young man.

"Are you staying at the hotel or just visiting?" the girl asked.

"I'm staying at the hotel for a few days, visiting from Chicago."

"Are you here for business or pleasure?"

I paused for a moment, sizing up the young couple. They must have suspected what I was up to when they saw me sitting alone again in the same tarty red dress. Plus, they probably saw me leave with the young Adonis two nights ago and noticed we got on the same elevator together. But they were a little too direct in their questions for my liking, and I decided to remain aloof until I could discern their motivations.

"A bit of both, I suppose," I said. "There's a lot to enjoy in this town."

"What line of work are you in?" the girl asked.

"I dabble in graphic design, but I've been branching out looking into some new opportunities while I'm in D.C.," I equivocated. "How about you guys? You seem a bit young to be mingling with this stuffy, overpriced crowd."

"Actually, Brodie's family owns the hotel," the girl said, smiling toward her husband.

I swiveled in my chair and peered at the young man with wide eyes.

"You're a *Marriott*?" I exclaimed.

"Shh," he said, motioning with his hand for me to talk more quietly. "I'm the great-grandson of J.W.," he nodded. "But I try to keep a low profile around here. I don't want people to think I expect any special favors or anything..."

"Oh?" I said, recognizing I might have hit the jackpot. "What were you two looking for coming to the bar tonight? I mean, this isn't the usual place young couples go to for some excitement in D.C."

"Actually," the girl said. "We wanted to make you a proposition. We noticed you've taken two different men up to your room the last couple of nights."

I crossed my arms defensively when I realized they'd been spying on me.

"What I choose to do in my own free time should be no concern of yours. And frankly, I find it unacceptable that a member of the hotel staff should accuse me of inappropriate behavior–"

"No, it's not like that," the girl said, placing her hand atop mine. "Brodie doesn't *work* here. We're just staying at the hotel for a few nights like you. We're not judging you in any way. In fact, we both find you highly attractive and wondered if you'd consider entertaining the two of us for the evening..."

"Entertaining?" I said, raising an eyebrow. "Aren't you guys a little young to be playing this game? You barely look old enough to be married."

"We're both twenty-one," the girl said. "Old enough to make our own decisions about who we'd like to have sex with."

The cat was out of the bag now, I thought. These guys sure didn't waste any time letting their desires be known.

"Have you talked this over?" I said, peering at both of them. "This isn't the sort of thing a young couple should take lightly. Introducing a third person into the mix can often incite feelings of jealousy and resentment."

"We've been talking it over," the girl said. "It's pretty much the *only* thing we've talked about for the last two days.

We both think you're insanely hot, and I've never been with another woman before. And Brodie's always fantasized about being in a menage..."

"Whoa," I chuckled. "You guys are going a little too fast for me. You do realize I do this for..."

"A *living*?" the girl smiled. "We kind of figured that out. That's not going to be a problem for the two of us. It's not like Brodie doesn't have money..."

"Okay," I said, not bothering to tell them this wasn't my full-time job. "It's a bit unconventional, but I'm up for if you guys are. Do you prefer my room or yours?"

"We're staying in the Presidential Suite on the top floor," Brodie said. "It's got a bit more room to move around, and a King-size bed."

"I guess that settles it then," I smiled. "My room's only got a Queen, and something tells me we're going to need the extra room to keep the three of us properly amused."

I motioned toward the bartender to bring me the bill, but when he approached the counter, Brodie indicated for him to put it on his room tab, and the three of us exited toward the hotel lobby.

When we got in the elevator, the girl held out her hand to me and smiled.

"I'm Emily, by the way. There's no need for us to be so formal. I mean since we're going to be getting to know each other pretty well shortly."

"Jade," I said, holding out my hand and clasping each of their sweaty hands separately. It was obvious that this was the first time either one of them had done something like this before. Whether they were sweating out of nervousness or excitement, I couldn't be sure. But I was certainly aware that a *different* part of me was getting wet thinking about all the fun I was about to have teaching these young kids about the pleasures of three-way sex.

When we reached the top floor and Brodie unlocked the door to his guest suite, my mouth practically hit the floor when I saw the size of his room. Easily four times the size of my suite, it was equipped with a separate dining room with fireplace, a gigantic bedroom overlooking the grounds of the White House, and an ensuite washroom that was larger than most people's living rooms.

"Wow," I said, taking in the opulently appointed room. "You guys really know how to travel in style. It must be nice being the owner's son."

"It has it's perks," Brodie smiled, picking up a bottle of cognac resting on the large oversize in-room bar. "Would you like something to drink?"

"Sure," I nodded. "It looks like your minibar is stocked a little better than mine."

Brodie twisted off the top of the decanter and poured me a glass of the burgundy-colored brandy, then handed it to me gently.

"Are you guys sure you haven't done this before?" I said, taking a sip of the sweet nectar. "Because you seem to have a pretty smooth operation going here."

"We're just used to traveling in luxury is all," Emily said, clinking her glass against mine. "Although we *have* had two full days to prepare for this eventuality."

"You were so sure I'd be that easy?"

"I'm not sure *easy* is the right word," Emily smiled. "You're a lot more high-class than most girls we see using this hotel."

"And here I thought I was the *first*," I chuckled, taking a big swig of my cognac.

"Do you want to freshen up?" Emily said. "Feel free to use the restroom if you need a few minutes."

"Thanks," I said, glancing toward the marble-lined washroom. "All this alcohol seems to going right through me."

When I entered the gleaming washroom and closed the cherry-wood door behind me, I glanced at myself in the huge mirror over the double-wide vanity, spreading my hands apart in the air.

Holy fuck, I mouthed at myself. *This is insane! What are the odds I'd run into the perfect couple on the second last night of my stay in DC? With the grandson of the founder of the Marriott hotel chain no less!*

After I took a minute to regain my composure, I disrobed and used a moist towel to freshen up my private parts, then I put on a silk robe hanging on the back of the door and reentered the main room. When I pushed open the door, I was surprised to see Emily and her husband already naked, lying beside one another on the oversize bed with the covers pulled overtop their torsos.

"You guys don't waste any time," I chuckled, looking at the young couple peering at me like a virgin awaiting her husband to join her in bed on their wedding night.

"We've been anticipating this moment for two long days," Emily said. "We didn't want to waste a precious moment."

"Alright then," I said, dropping my robe onto the floor as I approached the bed, revealing my naked body. "Let's get this party started."

"Huh!" Emily gasped when she saw my large breasts and naked hips for the first time. Both of them ran their eyes shamelessly over me like a kid in a candy store, and I noticed the bedspread over Brodie's midsection already tenting in excitement.

"Were you guys planning on letting me in there with

you, or were you going to cover yourselves up like shrinkwrap the whole time?"

"Um, okay," Emily said, pulling down the corner of the bedspread on her side and shifting over closer to her husband.

I smiled when I saw that she wanted first dibs on me and I strutted around the bed, swiveling my hips and bouncing my breasts to raise their excitement. When I reached Emily's side, I pulled the bedsheets down to the far end of the bed, exposing both of their naked bodies. Emily was about average height, but her body had the soft, supple flesh of a teenager, with nary a blemish to be found on her pale skin and perky breasts naturally pressed together from the buoyant elastin of an adolescent. Her pussy was shaved as smooth as a baby's bottom, and I smiled when I realized how much time she'd probably spent preparing her body for this moment. Her husband had an equally svelte figure, with a light dusting of hair on his hard pecs and six-pack abs, punctuated by a seven-inch hard-on flapping up against his belly button.

Oh, to be twenty years old again, I sighed.

I hadn't had sex with anyone this young in a long time, and I could feel the wetness accumulating on the outer fringes of my pussy as I licked my lips in anticipation.

"Where shall we get started?" I said, peering at their two quivering bodies. "You both look good enough to eat."

"Wherever you prefer," Emily said with a slight waver in her voice. "We've got all evening."

"Glad to hear," I said, crawling in the bed next to her then lifting up my knee to straddle her hips with my dripping pussy.

I leaned forward, pressing my tits hard against hers, swallowing her mouth in mine as I thrust my tongue deep into her cavity. She moaned in my mouth, encircling her tongue with mine as she rocked her hips and upper body, awkwardly trying to rub her skin against mine. I could feel her hardening teats pressing against the soft flesh of my breasts, and after a few minutes of humping our bodies together, I tilted my head a few inches lower, sucking her bullets into my mouth one at a time.

"*Oh my God*," she panted as I rolled my tongue around her tips, squeezing her firm breasts with my hands.

While I lavished her tits with my expert sucking, I glanced over at Brodie lying next to us out of the corner of my eyes, expecting him to be jackhammering his raging hard-on in excitement. But he was so gobsmacked by what I was doing to his wife, he simply lay back with eyes as wide as saucers watching me fuck her like no one had done before.

As Emily's chest rose and fell in increasing excitement from my ministrations, my pussy began to drip between her legs and she grabbed the sides of my buttocks, trying to press her mound harder against mine. But in my position sitting on top of her hips, there was no way for her more sensitive parts to make contact, and after teasing her for another ten minutes, I decided to spare her any further suffering and shifted my weight a little lower, spreading her legs apart. I glanced at her neat and bare pussy and shook my head at how unspoiled and symmetrical everything looked.

"Are you guys *sure* you're eighteen?" I said, peering at her gorgeous vulva. "Because you both look too perfect to be even *married* to one another."

"Good genes, I guess," Emily purred as she raised her knees, inviting me to move closer to her glistening snatch.

"Mmm," I nodded, noticing the head of Brodie's cock

dripping a long string of precum down onto his fluttering belly.

"I think Emily needs a little attention first," I said, smiling over toward him. "But feel free to get started without us. I'll get to you soon enough."

As I pressed Emily's knees higher up toward her chest, angling her flaring snatch toward me, I lowered my face onto her pretty cunt and began slurping her juices into my mouth. When Brodie saw me go down on his wife, he suddenly grabbed his pole and began beating it furiously while I tickled Emily's folds. As I sucked her lips loudly into my mouth, I peered up and saw her tilting her jaw down onto the top of her chest while she watched me eating her out.

"Oh my God," she panted. "You're so beautiful, Jade. I love watching you suck my pussy."

"So does your *husband*, evidently," I smiled, peering over at Brodie fapping his dick like a twelve-year-old who'd just discovered the joy of playing with his hard willie.

Emily threaded her hands behind her knees, pulling her legs up closer toward her head as her vulva tilted further up. I could see the nub of her clit pushing out of its hood like a ripe fruit waiting to be plucked. The look of desperation on her face was all I needed to move my head a little higher, and I swallowed her pearl in my mouth, sucking it hard as I twirled my tongue over her hard bean. As she grunted and threw her head back, I could feel the juices pouring out of her slit, dripping all the way down the front of my chin over my chest and my swelling breasts and nipples.

"Fuck yes," she growled. "Eat my cunt, Jade. Make me come all over your pretty face. I never dreamed it could be this good."

As I listened to Emily's breathing escalating in pitch and

urgency, I slipped two fingers into her slit and curled them toward her G-spot, feeling her pussy beginning to tent in preparation for an impending orgasm.

"Yes baby," I murmured. "Cum for me. Let me feel you clamping down over my fingers and mashing your pussy into my face. You're so soft and sweet."

"Yes, Jade," she began to wail. "I'm going to come all over your pretty face. Oh God, Oh God, Oh God..."

Suddenly, she screamed at the top of her lungs as her entire body began lurching wildly in her bent-over fetal position. It took every bit of my focus to keep my mouth from slipping off her burning jewel as she jerked and spasmed in my mouth. I pressed my face harder against her vulva and held her softly until her contractions started to ebb. When she finally stopped coming, we both relaxed our grip and peered over at Brodie who had a sheepish grin on his face, with long ropes of translucent cum streaked all over his abdomen and upper chest.

4

———

After Emily had recovered from her powerful orgasm, I noticed her husband's pecker had deflated somewhat, lying flat on his belly like an overcooked sausage.

"Are you still raring to go, chipper?" I said. "Or do you need a bit of time to recharge your batteries?"

"Sorry," he said. "I guess I got a bit carried away. When Em came, I couldn't hold back any longer."

"No worries," I chuckled at his youthful exuberance. "I'm pretty sure we can find a way to raise the flag on your pole with a few other distractions. Are you ready for a little *two-way* action this time, Emily?

"*Fuck* yes," she said, sitting up excitedly.

"Good, because my private parts could use a little attention also."

"Do you want me to–" she said, peering down at my dripping pussy.

"Maybe later," I replied, seeing that she wanted to go down on me. "Right now, I want to fuck you right proper. I haven't had a pretty young thing like you to screw in a long time. Spread your legs for me. I'm going to stimulate you with a *different* part of my body this time."

As Emily's eyes widened realizing what I had in mind, she lifted her right leg high up above her body until it was angled ninety degrees in the air, showing her bare cunny. I took one look at her glistening snatch and straddled her hips once again, this time with one knee positioned just below her pussy and one over the left side of her hip with my ass facing in Brodie's direction.

This ought to get his motor running again, I smiled as I lowered my steaming pussy onto Emily's sex.

When our vulvas touched, she gasped and reached out to squeeze my tits, playing with my hardening teats.

"Do you like that, Emily?" I said. "Do you like the feel of another woman's cunt rubbing up against your own?"

"God yes," she panted, pinching my nipples hard enough to make them hurt.

"You ain't seen nothing yet, baby," I purred, pulling her upturned leg between my tits as I pressed my pussy harder against hers.

I angled her body forty-five degrees to the side so Brodie could have a clearer view of our two pussies rubbing together, then I peered over my shoulder noticing his prick was bouncing back up in the air high above his belly button.

"You might want to try holding off pounding that thing for a little longer this time," I smiled. "That is, if you were hoping to get in on the action next time around."

"Definitely," he panted, staring at our pink snatches mashing together only a few inches from his face.

"Get ready, Emily," I said, peering up at his wife. "Because this is about to get a bit messy."

"I like messy," she mewed. "Mess me up anyway you

want, Jade. I want to experience everything you've got in your bag of tricks."

Ignoring her backhanded comment, I grabbed her leg and tilted my hips backward a few inches until our two mounds touched, feeling her hard nub roll over my own. When she felt our clits touch, she groaned and grabbed my hips, pulling me closer.

"Yeah, baby," I growled. "Can you feel my clit touching yours? Do you like mashing our cunnies together?"

"Yes," she panted, arching her chest up toward me as she lifted her face to peer more closely at our grinding pussies.

I pulled her head closer toward me and kissed her hard on the lips, and she reached around her upturned leg and my back, pressing our bodies closer together while she moaned into my mouth and twisting her shoulders as we flapped our tits together.

I heard a loud moan coming from behind me and wondered if Brodie was managing to keep his act together. It must have been near-impossible for him to keep his hands off his hard-on watching his wife in the embrace of an experienced older woman as they ground their pussies together.

But *his* needs were the last thing on my mind right now. As I began to feel my own pleasure rapidly beginning to rise from touching every surface of his pretty young wife's body pressing up against me, I wrapped my arms around her back with her upturned leg pointing up like a spear between us and moaned along with her as our tongues danced together in escalating ecstasy.

As I began to feel my orgasm rising up inside me like an oncoming freight train, I thought it was only fair to give my partner fair warning.

"I'm going to cum all over your pretty pussy, Emily," I said, pulling away from her momentarily.

"Oh, God yes," she panted. "I'm almost there with you. I want to feel your hot pussy coming with me. Brodie, are you watching this?"

"Are you *kidding* me?" he said. "I haven't been able to keep my eyes off the two of you ever since you touched your pussies together."

"I hope that's the *only* part you've been using to enjoy the show," I said. "Because I have plans for that nice hard dick of yours when I'm done here."

"I'll definitely be up for that when you guys finish," he panted. "I haven't been this hard in ages!"

I smiled at the thought of him watching his wife getting fucked by a hot hooker, picturing his joystick overflowing with precum like a volcano about to erupt. The imagery only added to my excitement, and as the feeling of rising tension in my body passed the point of no return, I pulled Emily harder toward me as I began gushing all over her ass and our tightly compressed pussies.

"*What the–*" Emily gasped, flinging her eyes open at the unexpected sensation of me squirting between her legs. "*Unghhhh,*" she groaned in a long guttural moan as her body began twitching wildly again in the throes of her own orgasm.

With her mouth, tits, pussy, and leg all pressed up tightly against me while we came together, the sensation was like nothing I'd felt before and I couldn't help screaming along with her in the throes of the most powerful orgasm I'd had in eons. As we held each other tightly, jerking and moaning in excited ecstasy, I could feel my juices spraying all over her leg and the bedspread while my pussy flexed and convulsed for almost a full minute. With my ass angled in Brodie's direction, I was sure some of my spray was squirting in the direction of his upturned cock, and I wondered if he'd be able to hold off cumming from the combination of exciting sensations he was witnessing.

At least he's going to be plenty *lubricated* when his turn comes, I smiled.

As Emily's and my contractions slowly began to subside, we loosened our grip on each other and kissed softly while we panted into each other's mouths. The feeling of her upturned leg still resting between our faces and sweaty chests was strange but wonderful, and I shook my head at her youthful, effortless flexibility.

Thank you, Lord, I muttered to myself, *for placing these two kids in my path this week.*

This turning tricks business was getting harder and harder to escape by the moment.

———

After Emily and I untangled our bodies and lay down on the bed, we peered over at Brodie, who had an expectant look in his eyes as his dick throbbed in a rapid flapping motion high above his abdomen. It was coated in a thick layer of precum and my own juices dripping down the side of his shaft, but at least he was still hard and eager.

"Good boy," I said, peering over at his delicious-looking organ. "Something tells me your husband could use a little attention of his own right about now. Do you mind if I give him a quickie while you rest up and recover for a few minutes?"

"Not in the least," Emily said. "I've been wanting to watch another woman giving him a blowjob for a long time."

"Only a blowjob?" I said."

"I've got something *else* in mind for him when you're done there," she smiled. "Just try not to come baby while

Jade's sucking your dick. I want to feel you cumming inside me before we finish up here tonight."

"I'll try, honey," he said. "But I almost popped off just watching you guys. I don't know if I'll be able to–"

I rolled over and popped his popsicle into my mouth, tasting the combination of his youthful spunk and my own juices dripping down over his head. His dick pulsed, and I felt another small jet of precum dribbling out of his slit, and I grabbed his organ hard with both hands, trying to prevent his full release from spilling out.

"Oh *Godddd*," he groaned, watching my head bobbing up and down his purple pole.

"Do you like that baby?" Emily purred, watching her husband getting a blowjob from a perfect stranger. "Do you like getting sucked off by another woman while I watch?"

"Fuck yes," he grunted as he humped my face with his flapping drumstick.

"Just don't come in her mouth, okay? Because that would be impolite. Besides, I want you to save the best for me. I'm rubbing my pussy watching you get sucked off."

Brodie turned his head to peer at his wife with her legs spread wide apart and her fingers embedded in her pussy as she thrust them in and out of her hole.

"Fuck *me*," he panted, struggling harder to hold off exploding in my mouth.

"Yes, baby," she groaned. "I will soon enough. I just want to watch your cock twisting in Jade's mouth a little longer."

I began to twirl my tongue around the sensitive ridge of Brodie's bulging crown, and he groaned louder, lifting his hips off the bed. It was clear that he wanted me to go down further on his cock, and although I knew how to take a man's penis into my throat, I resisted the temptation knowing that if I did, he'd lose any chance of maintaining control any further.

But that didn't stop me from lowering my mouth far enough to meet the top of my hands grasping his dick hand-over-hand, and as his moaning and humping action began to escalate toward an impending climax, I suddenly popped my mouth off his flexing head, watching his joystick jerking wildly as he continued humping the air, desperate to get off.

"I think your husband needs to finish his business before he has an aneurysm," I said, watching the precum pouring out of his slit all the way down the side of his hard-on as his balls pulled up tightly toward the base of his pole.

"I think so too," Emily said. "Come over here, baby. I have an idea where all *three* of us can have some fun together. Jade, do you mind lying down with your head closer to the baseboard? I've always wanted to see what it's like eating another woman's pussy..."

"My pleasure," I said, not quite sure what she had in mind but eager to see Brodie get in on the action.

As I lay down as Emily instructed, she turned her body around and straddled by stomach, then shifted down a few inches until her pussy wavered a few inches above my face.

"Brodie," she continued instructing her husband. "I want you to position yourself behind my ass and above Jade's face while you fuck me from behind. That way you can watch both of us sucking each other's pussies while you come inside me. Just try to hold out long enough to come along with me. I want to feel the three of us coming together if possible."

"I'll try, baby," he said, eagerly shifting his body into position directly over my head.

I could see his glistening pole coated with a combination of his precum, my saliva, and my pussy juices dripping over his balls mere inches above my face, and I was tempted to take them into my mouth, but I was mindful of Emily's wishes to hold off so we could all enjoy the experience together.

"Okay, baby," Emily said. "Sink your dick into me as I lower my pussy onto Jade's face. Watch me eat her cunt while you fuck my pussy. I want to feel you squirting inside me while she sprays all over my face."

"Fuck yes," he groaned, burying his organ deep into his wife's hole.

I found it incredibly hot watching his cock sliding in and out of Emily's pussy just inches above my face, and as I felt her juices beginning to drip onto my forehead, I lifted my mouth closer to her snatch, sucking her clit into my mouth.

"Oh God, baby," Emily hissed. "I can feel your cock deep inside me while Jade's sucking my pussy. Pound my ass while she eats my cunt."

"*Nnngh*," Brodie groaned, clearly enjoying the combination of the sensations watching the of two of us sixty-nining underneath him while his wife urged him on.

Meanwhile, Emily was doing an expert job of her own sucking my pussy as she twirled her tongue in circles around my flaring bud while she sucked it in and out of her mouth like a raw oyster. As I began to feel my pleasure inexorably rising once again, I rolled my hips harder against her face to signal my appreciation, which caused her to moan even louder as I sucked her twat equally as hard.

If this was her first time making love to a woman, I thought, she's got an exciting future ahead of her experimenting with more swinging adventures with her young husband.

With the three of us moaning and squealing like a pack of wolves, I watched Brodie's testicles progressively rising and tightening as he pounded his dick harder against Emily's ass. It was obvious that he wasn't going to be able to hold out much longer, and I slapped the sides of Emily's ass with my hands as I sucked her button in and out of my mouth more forcefully. As she began to wail louder leading up to another climax, I reached up and clasped Brodie's balls with my two hands, squeezing them tightly while he thrust his hips hard against Emily's ass in one last powerful thrust.

As Emily's hips began quaking in the midst of another intense orgasm, her husband grunted above us, finally emptying his seed deep into her chasm as I felt my own orgasm begin to overtake me. Feeling all of my sexual tension releasing in a sudden explosion, I clamped my thighs tightly around Emily's head, muffling her moans while I gushed all over her face and breasts compressed against my chest.

It must have been an incredible sight for Brodie to witness all this from his perfect vantage point perched above the two of us, watching us writhing and squirting into each other's pussies. While I watched the muscles of his perineum flexing along with his wife's in a long, simultaneous climax, I couldn't help smiling at how things had taken such a strange turn this week.

I had no idea being a hooker could be this much fun, and I was already looking forward to my final night's stay at this magical hotel.

5

———

Thankfully, my last day of client meetings was blissfully short, and I got back to the hotel early to prepare for my final night of hustling. Emily and Brodie had left me two thousand bucks for our two hours together in the Presidential Suite, and I was eager to see if I could up the ante even further tonight. This business of selling my body for money was starting to become addictive, and I wondered what the upper limit might be for my services.

When I walked into the Regis Bar around 8 p.m., it was busier than usual, and I had to fend off a bevy of eager young studs who clearly didn't have the means to satisfy my newly elevated standards. After last night's tryst with Brodie and Emily, I was on the lookout for another well-to-do couple that might be hoping to spice up their marriage, or at least a hot older woman who was curious about experimenting with some easy pussy.

As I peered into the bar mirror scanning the room while sipping my martini, I noticed a pretty brunette about my age sitting in a corner of the lounge watching me intently. She didn't seem interested in making eye contact with me so much as amusing herself watching all the young men at the bar trying to pick me up. After an hour or so, she sauntered up to the counter, taking a seat next to me.

"Hey," she casually said, motioning for the bartender to bring her a drink.

"Thank heavens," I sighed. "I could use a little female company to divert the attention of all these overeager playboys."

"I noticed," she said, ordering a Manhattan when the bartender came to the counter. "I thought you could use a little help. But you can't blame them really. You kind of stand out like bullseye in this dark bar."

"Because of my bright red dress?"

"That, and because you're probably the hottest woman who's come into this place in months."

"Thanks," I said, appraising her expensive and perfectly-tailored wool suit. "You don't look so bad yourself. What brings you to this wolf's den all alone on a Thursday night? You don't look like one of those political types, and you sure as hell aren't a tourist."

"I'm in security," she said. "There's a lot of important people to protect in this town."

"Really?" I said, intrigued by her low-key demeanor. "You mean like Secret Service or something like that?"

"Something like that. I'm not really at liberty to disclose my sponsor. I'm sure you can understand."

"Of course," I chuckled. "It seems that *everybody's* got something to hide around here."

"What about you?" she said. "You don't exactly look like a typical Washington lawyer or a political aide. Not in *that* clingy outfit, at least. No wonder all the men are swarming to you like bees to honey. You're not leaving much to the imagination."

"Oh?" I said, noticing her lingering a little longer than usual as she ran her eyes up and down my body. "Is that what you were doing all this time from the other side of the room? Undressing me with your eyes?"

"Well, you *are* a pretty comely distraction. Plus, you didn't seem to be too interested in satisfying the *guys*."

"I guess I'm just waiting for the right prospect to come along," I teased.

"What would it take to entice you off this stool? Because I'm definitely interested."

"What are you offering?" I demurred.

"*Oh*," the woman said, taking a deep sip of her cocktail. "Is *that* your game? I do happen to be carrying a little extra cash with me tonight. I'm sure I can make it worth your while."

"I'm sure you could," I said, peering at her curvy legs hanging over the edge of her stool. "I've got a room upstairs if you're interested."

"Oh I'm *definitely* interested," she said. "I'm Tess, by the way."

"Jade," I said, shaking her surprisingly firm hand.

"Lead the way, Jade," Tess said, extending her arm in the direction of the hotel lobby. "I'm eager to sample your wares."

When we got in the elevator to head up to my room, we both stood facing the brass door peering at our reflection in the metallic surface. There was something oddly aloof about this woman, but that just piqued my interest even more. I was definitely ready to experiment with a more experienced woman for a change, and I could feel my panties get wetter and wetter the closer we got to my floor.

When we entered my room and closed the door behind us, Tess paused for me to make the first move, and I pressed her up against the wall, hiking her knee-length skirt up her thighs. As I reached around to grab her firm ass, she unzipped the back of my dress while swirling her tongue around my mouth. By the time we staggered over to the side of my bed, we'd left a trail of undergarments on the floor, breathing heavily as we both fell onto the mattress.

Not bothering to pull the bedsheets down, Tess flipped me over and straddled my ass, rubbing her wet pussy over my bare cheeks. It felt exciting to have another woman taking charge for a change, and as she spread her juices over my cool skin, I felt my nipples hardening as she jerked my body up and down the bedspread with her aggressive humping action.

After a few minutes, she stood up and retrieved her purse from the console opposite the bed. I looked at her with pinched eyebrows, wondering what could motivate her to pause just as things were starting to get hot and heavy.

"Do you mind if I add a little sex toy to our playtime?" she said, reaching into her purse.

"Not at all," I purred. "I've got quite a stash at home myself."

But when she pulled out a huge pink strap-on dildo, my eyes bulged, surprised at the boldness of her request.

"Were you looking to be the recipient or the *user* of that weapon?" I said.

"That ass looks far too *delicious* for me to pass up," she said, staring at my upturned, glistening cheeks. "You don't mind, do you? I mean, I thought you guys were up for anything?"

"You *guys*?" I said, slightly annoyed at her intimation that I was a run-of-the-mill hooker.

"Ladies of the night, call girl, whatever you high-end hookers call yourself these days."

"If the price is right," I said, no longer feigning innocence. "You can call me anything you like or have me anyway you like."

"Mmm," she said, strapping the harness around her hips then flicking her hips to send the protruding phallus twirling in circles. "Assume the position. I want to fuck that sweet ass and listen to you moan."

"Yes please," I said, angling my buttocks higher in the air to give her a view of my glistening snatch. "Fuck me with your big cock. Make me cum with your lady dick."

For the first time in four nights, I felt myself play-acting to satisfy my client's prurient interests, rather than expressing my genuine desire. Still, there was something exciting about her direct and aggressive manner, and I was happy to play along.

"Do you like that?" she said, kneeling on the bed behind me, slapping her hard phallus against the sides of my cheeks. "Do you like getting fucked by ladyboys? I bet you've tried just about everything in your line of work."

"You'd be surprised," I said, not prepared to tell her how much of a relative novice I was.

"Do you want it up the ass or your *other* hole?" she said, taunting me.

"It'll cost you an extra G if you want to fuck me up the ass," I said, getting fully into role now. "Whatever strikes your fancy–have at it."

Tess grabbed the dildo with her right hand and swiped it up and down my dripping vulva to lubricate it, then she placed the head of the plastic cock around my bunghole, teasing me as my ass quivered in hesitation. I wasn't generally into anal sex, but at least in this case it would be with something that couldn't pass along any diseases.

But when she lowered the dildo further down my perineum and began to enter my pussy, I breathed a sigh of relief. I'd far rather she fuck me in a place where I could *enjoy* the process, and as she began to push her hips against my butt, I leaned back against her, not giving her a chance to have second thoughts. As she began to pound me with loud slapping noises and the sloshing sound of the artificial cock hammering in and out of my increasingly wet pussy, I peered back at her, noticing the unmistakable look of rising ecstasy on her face. Even though she wasn't getting direct stimulation on her erogenous parts, it was obvious she'd been harboring this fantasy for quite some time and was getting off simply at the idea of fucking me with a cock.

I reached underneath me and spread my hand, pressing my fingers against her mound and she angled her hips, slipping my fingers under the base of the harness where I could feel her warm pussy and protruding clit. I pinched my fingers on either side of her bulb as she continued pounding me with her dildo, sliding her nub in the crease as she began to pant more loudly.

"*Fuck yes*, bitch," she said, dispensing with any prior niceties. "Rub my clit while I pound your ass. Make me come with your pretty fingers. I'm going to dump my cum deep inside you."

Now who's going over the top with the play-acting? I thought. No matter though, I suppose that's what most johns want from their hookers anyway: to live out their wildest fantasies with a perfect stranger who'll keep their secret from their lovers and spouses.

"Yeah, baby," I panted, beginning to get turned on from our little role-playing game. "Fuck me with your big thumper. I'm going to gush all over your balls when you come inside me."

"God damn, girl," she said, approaching the height of her pleasure. "You really know how to hit all the right buttons."

"You have *no* idea," I said, beginning to feel the familiar pangs of pressure building up inside me. "Come with me baby. Let me feel you spraying your load inside my burning twat."

"Fuck yes," she growled. "Keep rubbing me there. I'm going to come. Oh God, I'm going to come so hard–"

Somehow, the thought of this sexy woman living out her wildest fantasies, about to have an incredible orgasm while I diddled her clit under her faux penis, was a huge rush for me, and as she began grunting in the throes of a powerful climax, I couldn't hold back the floodgates any longer, gushing all over her flapping pussy and my hand squeezing her clit. When she felt me spraying all over her cunt, she grabbed the sides of my ass and humped me harder, wailing in delight at my special skills.

Damn straight, I smiled to myself. *See if you can find another hooker who can play-act that while you're fucking her up the ass.*

When she finally pulled out of me and flopped down onto the bed beside me, she peered over at me with a huge grin.

"Holy shit, girl," she panted. "You really *like* what you do for a living, don't you?"

"I'm not gonna lie," I smiled. "It definitely has its surprises. But when I'm with a hot number like you, I like to have a little fun of my *own*."

"That was definitely worth the price of admission," she sighed. "How much do I owe you?"

"I don't have a set fee," I said, playing coy. "Whatever you think I'm worth. But I'm pretty sure you got your money's worth."

"Fuck yeah," she said, getting up off the bed and opening her purse to fish around for her payment.

But when she pulled out a small leather case and flipped it open to reveal a police badge, my heart sunk into my throat.

"You really should be more careful where you ply your wares," she said. "I'm surprised you didn't already get picked up before tonight."

"Was I *that* obvious?" I said, sitting up and pulling the covers up over my torso, suddenly feeling exposed.

"The tight dress, the furtive looks, the suggestive comments. It didn't take a genius to figure out what you were up to from the other side of the room."

"Are you planning to take me in?" I said, suddenly regretting my little side-adventure this week.

"By all rights, I should," she said. "But something tells me you're new to this game. I'm going to let you off with a warning this time. Besides, you gave me more than I bargained for, so we'll call it even. Just don't let me see you working this side of town anytime again soon."

"Actually, this was going to be my last night in DC anyways," I said. "I wasn't really planning to do this any longer after I got back to my home town."

I glanced up at the sexy detective, noticing that she hadn't bothered to remove her glistening strap-on dildo yet.

"But since I'm here for the rest of the night, I don't suppose you'd like to stay for a little more fun? I was thinking of some *other* ways we could put that thing to good use. *Gratis* this time, of course."

She peered at me for a long moment as a Cheshire Cat grin formed on her lips.

"If *you* don't tell, *I* won't tell," she said, ripping off her harness and pouncing on top of me, grinding her slippery pussy against mine.

Fucking eh, I thought as she leaned in to push her tongue down my throat. *I dodged a bullet this time. Maybe this turning tricks thing isn't all it's cracked up to be after all.*

As I rolled over to pull Tess on top of me, I smiled feeling her warm tits rubbing against mine.

Still, it was a fun little diversion while it lasted. And I've made double the money this week for four times the fun.

Ready for more erotic chills and thrills? Order the next exciting volume in Jade's Erotic Adventures:

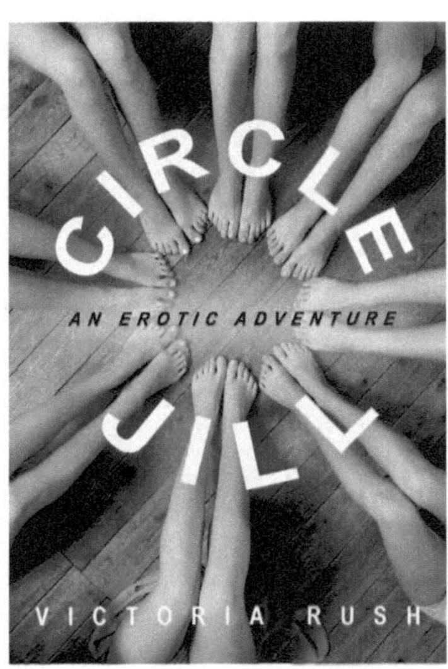

Some girls just need a little extra encouragement to come out of their shells...

www.ingramcontent.com/pod-product-compliance
Lightning Source LLC
Chambersburg PA
CBHW051713180726
48283CB00004B/1333